I.Q. GOES TO THE LIBRARY

By Mary Ann Fraser

SUNDAY

WALKER & COMPANY ✦ NEW YORK

First published in the United States of America in 2003 by
Walker Publishing Company, Inc.

Published simultaneously in Canada by Fitzhenry and Whiteside, Markham, Ontario L3R 4T8

For information about permission to reproduce selections from
this book, write to Permissions, Walker & Company, 435 Hudson Street, New York, New York 10014

Library of Congress Cataloging-in-Publication Data
Fraser, Mary Ann.
I.Q. goes to the library / Mary Ann Fraser.
p. cm.
Summary: After going to the library with Mrs. Furber's class every day of Library Week, I.Q., the class pet, hopes
to take out a funny book with his own library card.
ISBN 0-8027-8877-7 — ISBN 0-8027-8878-5 (lib. bdg.)
[1. Libraries—Fiction. 2. Pets—Fiction. 3. Schools—Fiction.] I. Title.

PZ7.F86455Io 2003
[E]—dc21
2003045047

The artist used pencil, gouache, and pen and ink
on Strathmore paper to create the illustrations for this book.

Book design by Victoria Allen

Visit Walker & Company's Web site at www.walkeryoungreaders.com

Printed in Hong Kong

2 4 6 8 10 9 7 5 3 1

To Barbara Leighty,
a librarian and friend

MONDAY

On Monday our teacher, Mrs. Furber, said, "Students, this is Library Week. Every day this week our class will be going to the library."

Within the illustration, on the bulletin board:

LIBRARY
WEEK

MRS. BINDER'S
REMINDER #1

A bookbag is
a must
to protect books
from rain,
dirt, and dust.

AUTHOR
VISIT

ANNOUNCING
BOOKMARK
CONTEST

I.Q. had never been to the library.
He didn't want to stay behind in the
classroom. He wanted to go with the
other students.

Mrs. Binder, the librarian, welcomed the class.
"Today is Reading-Corner Day," she said. "Come have a
seat by the big chair, and I will read a book to you."

The story made I.Q. laugh until his eyes watered and his tail curled. He wanted to take the book back to the classroom with him.

Mrs. Binder explained that books had to be checked out. "Class," she said, "if you complete a permission slip, I will give you a library card. Then you can check out a book."

I.Q. wanted to check out the funny book Mrs. Binder had just read, but the book had already been reshelved. The library was such a large place. I.Q. was glad he still had four days to find the funny book.

SIMPLE CONSTRUCTIONS

THE LOST BOOK

HE LOST BOOK

MOUNTAIN CONQUESTS

MRS. BINDER'S REMINDER #2
To keep books neat when you read, don't drink or eat.

TUESDAY

On Tuesday I.Q. came ready to explore the library.
There were rows and rows of videos, CDs, DVDs,
audiocassettes, magazines, puppets, and newspapers.

And there were *so* many books. Some books had hard covers and some had paper covers. Some were easy readers and others had long chapters and small print. There were books on shelves and books on racks that spun.

"Today is Puppet Day," announced Mrs. Binder. "Who would like to help me with the puppets?" I.Q. raised his paw first.

MRS. BINDER'S REMINDER #3

A whispering voice is the best choice.

The puppet fit perfectly. As Mrs. Binder read the book, I.Q. acted it out. When the story was over it was time to go back to the classroom. I.Q counted on his paw. Only three days left to find the book.

WEDNESDAY

On Wednesday I.Q. went to the book area marked NONFICTION. He was amazed at all the different topics.

Ratsy Ross
Patriot

Hamster Houdini
Magician

Mouseart
Composer

In the BIOGRAPHY section I.Q. found a book on famous rodents. It looked interesting, but he thought the book Mrs. Binder had read on the first day was funnier. He decided to keep looking for it.

"Could everyone come over to the audio table?" asked Mrs. Binder. "This is Books-on-Tape Day."

I.Q. liked the earphones. They were very comfortable.

Soon the story was over, and I.Q. realized it was time to go. He was getting worried. There were only two days left to find the funny book.

THURSDAY

On Thursday I.Q. discovered a section of books marked FICTION.

He realized the books all had stories invented by the author.

Some had drawings in them, some had photographs, and some only had words.

I.Q. liked the picture books the best. They made him feel BIG.

When he was done with a book he was careful to put it back exactly where he found it.

Mrs. Binder gathered all of the students at a table. "Today is Bookmark Day. Bookmarks help you mark your place in a book without ruining it. You each can make one."

I.Q. had some problems making his bookmark. By the time he had unstuck his tail, Mrs. Furber had come to fetch the class. Most of the other students had already checked out a book. I.Q. had only one day left to find his book and get a library card.

FRIDAY

On Friday when the class came to the library, Mrs. Binder said, "Today is Computer Day. It is also our last day of Library Week." Mrs. Binder showed the students how she used the computer to find a book. When she was done, I.Q. scrambled down to try.

1. Author
2. Title
3. Subject

Enter: 1

I.Q. pushed the mouse until it was where he wanted it. Then he jumped on the mouse to make it click.

Enter th
Title : A

Next he danced on the keys to type in the title of the book he wanted.

Finally all the information he needed was on the screen. He wrote it down and hurried over to the shelf.

At last, I.Q. had found the funny book. The tricky part was getting the book onto Mrs. Binder's desk.

Carefully he filled out the permission slip for the library card. But there on the bottom was a line that said "Parent/Guardian signature." I.Q. didn't know what to do.

Just then the bell rang and Mrs. Furber came to get her class. I.Q. felt terrible. He was the only student without a book or library card.

"Excuse me, Mrs. Furber," said Mrs. Binder, "I have a book with an incomplete permission slip here."

Mrs. Furber looked at the name on the permission slip. "Since I take care of him, I guess I am his guardian. I can sign that," she said.

DUE DATE

MRS. BINDER'S
REMINDER #7

Return or renew
when your
book is due.

I.Q. beamed from whisker to whisker as Mrs. Binder made him a library card. He wrote his name on it very neatly so everyone would know it was his.

SATURDAY

On Saturday I.Q. was alone all day in the classroom. But for once he didn't mind. He read his book over and over, laughing until his eyes watered and his tail curled.

SUNDAY

On Sunday he imagined all of the other things
he would check out with his new library card.

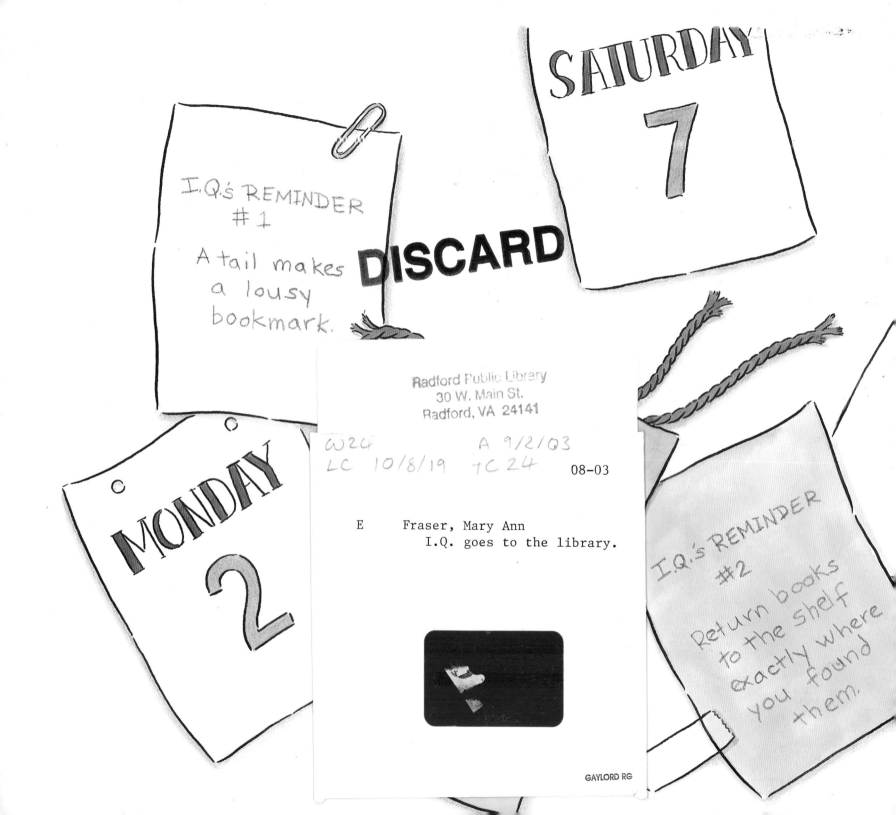